W9-DCU-043

Hannibal's Noisy Day

A fantasy story
in a familiar setting

This edition first published in 2009
by Sea-to-Sea Publications
Distributed by Black Rabbit Books
P.O. Box 3263
Mankato, Minnesota 56002

Text © Anne Adeney 2005, 2009
Illustration © Christina Bretschneider 2005

Printed in China

A CIP catalog record for this book is
available from the Library of Congress.

ISBN 978-1-59771-159-3

9 8 7 6 5 4 3 2 1

Published by arrangement with the
Watts Publishing Group Ltd, London.

Series Editor: Jackie Hamley
Series Advisors: Dr. Linda Gambrell,
Dr. Barrie Wade, Dr. Hilary Minns
Series Designer: Peter Scoulding

For my niece Hanna who loves all kinds of animals! – C.B.

Hannibal's Noisy Day

Written by
Anne Adeney

Illustrated by
Christina Bretschneider

SEA-TO-SEA
Mankato Collingwood London

Anne Adeney

"My favorite pet was 'Rainbow', my chameleon. My four children had lots of pets, too. The hamster was the smallest, and the noisiest!"

Christina Bretschneider

"I live with my two cats, Mimi and Biene. I love drawing all kinds of animals but I have never owned a hamster!"

It was morning.

Hannibal the hamster shut his eyes. "It's time for me to sleep now."

Then Jacob's alarm clock rang:
COCK-A-DOODLE-DOOOO!

"Be quiet!" said Hannibal.

"I'm trying to sleep!"

"Jacob is going to school,"
said Hannibal.

"Time for me to sleep."

Then the mailman arrived:
DING-DONG!

Ding-Dong

"Be quiet!" said Hannibal.

"I'm trying to sleep!"

Hannibal shut his eyes. Then
Grandma started cleaning:
BRMM-BRMM!

Brmm

"Be quiet!" said Hannibal.

"I'm trying to sleep!"

Hannibal went to sleep.

Then the baby started to cry:

"WAAH-WAAH!"

"Be quiet!" said Hannibal.

"I'm trying to sleep!"

"I'll sleep now," said Hannibal.

An ambulance went by:

NEE-NAA! NEE-NAA!

"Be quiet!" said Hannibal.

"I'm trying to sleep!"

Later on, Kelly came in.
"Wake up, Hannibal!"
said Kelly. "Let's play!"

"Be quiet!" said Hannibal.
"I'm trying to sleep!"

When Dad came home, he cut
the grass: ZROOM-ZROOM!

Then Mom put the radio on:
"LA-LA-LA-LA-LAAAA!"

"BE QUIET!" said Hannibal.

"I'm trying to sleep.

Why are you so *noisy*?"

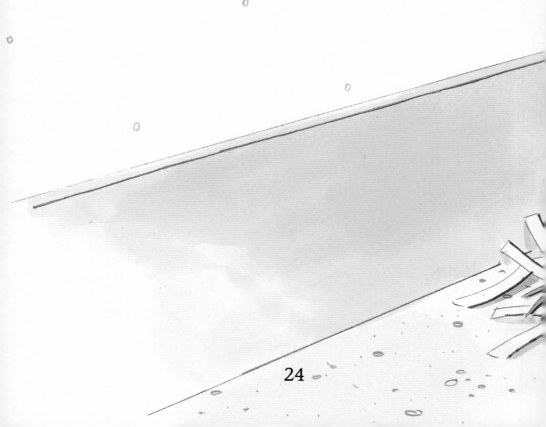

25

At last, everyone sat down to eat.

Hannibal could have a good sleep.

When Hannibal woke up,

he saw his wheel.

clitter-clatter!

"*I can play now,*" he said:
CLITTER-CLATTER!

Notes for parents and teachers

READING CORNER has been structured to provide maximum support for new readers. The stories may be used by adults for sharing with young children. Primarily, however, the stories are designed for newly independent readers, whether they are reading these books in bed at night, or in the reading corner at school or in the library.

Starting to read alone can be a daunting prospect. READING CORNER helps by providing visual support and repeating words and phrases, while making reading enjoyable. These books will develop confidence in the new reader, and encourage a love of reading that will last a lifetime!

If you are reading this book with a child, here are a few tips:

1. Make reading fun! Choose a time to read when you and the child are relaxed and have time to share the story.

2. Encourage children to reread the story, and to retell the story in their own words, using the illustrations to remind them what has happened.

3. Give praise! Remember that small mistakes need not always be corrected.

READING CORNER covers three grades of early reading ability, with three levels at each grade. Each level has a certain number of words per story, indicated by the number of bars on the spine of the book, to allow you to choose the right book for a young reader:

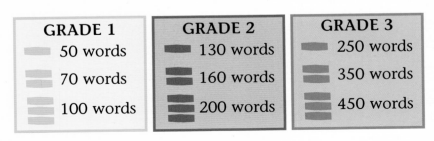

GRADE 1	GRADE 2	GRADE 3
50 words	130 words	250 words
70 words	160 words	350 words
100 words	200 words	450 words